Fabulous Friends

Storybook with Musical Microphone

Based on the series created by Michael Poryes and Rich Correll & Barry O'Brien

Contents

Reader's Digest
Children's Books®

Pleasantville, New York • Montréal, Québec • Bath, United Kingdom

Miley
Get Your Gum

After a Hannah Montana concert, Miley, Lilly and Robby hurried into a waiting limo. Robby was disguised as Hannah's security guard, and Lilly wore a red wig and carried a lap dog.

Robby tried to shut the door. "Clear the way people, superstar coming through!" he cried.

"And her jetset friend, Miss Lola Lof' Tanza," said Lilly. "Back off people! Don't make me release Thor!" Lilly held up the dog in a threatening manner and growled.

"Hannah! Hold up!"

"Oh no," said Miley. "It's Oliver."

I want you to see...

...the other side of me!

Uh-oh, it's Oliver.

Good dog! Oliver will think that I'm doing the licking!

Here's a token of my love, Hannah!

"Kiss my hand and I'll never wash it again!" said Oliver.

"Come on, Thor, make yourself useful," said Miley.

Thor licked Oliver's hand.

"Oh, baby, you're an animal!" said Oliver, peddling his bike alongside the limo. As he started to fall behind, he threw a bunch of flowers into the window.

The next day Oliver was at the beach shack telling a group of guys about his adventure.

"Hannah actually kissed this hand," said Oliver.

Chad went over to Oliver and chewed gum in his face.

Oliver got annoyed. "Chad, dude, you're getting spit on the Hannah hand!" he said.

Chad took out his wad of gum, slapped it on Oliver's Hannah hand and laughed like a fool.

"Take it off, dude!" Oliver cried.

Chad's gum brought back an awful memory from Oliver's nursery days. An annoying

Hannah licked this hand.
She licked it! She...ack, gum!

Look at the cutie widdle baby!

Ooops! There goes my gum!

Hannah, why are you upside down?
Oh, wait, I'M the one upside down.

Lilly! I mean, Lola! I can't see!

gum-chewing older woman with way too much makeup was leaning over his crib.

"Oh, little baby Ollie," cooed Aunt Harriet. "Aunt Harriet just wants to eat you up. You're so yummy."

Her gum fell out of her mouth and landed on baby Oliver, who started to scream and cry.

Oliver shook himself out of the flashback. "Ugh!"

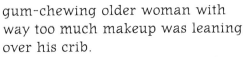

That night in the limo Miley took off her wig and said, "Oliver stared right into my eyes and never had a clue."

Hanging upside down from the roof, Oliver peered in at Miley, Lilly and Robby.

"Ahh!" cried Miley. She grabbed Thor and put him in front of her face. Robby put the wig back on her head.

"Wow, you're even more beautiful upside down," Oliver said.

"Look," Miley said, "I have a boyfriend."

Sorry, dude, you're on your own.

Oh, Oliver, you're the best!

Oliver looked stunned. "A boyfriend?" he said. "Then why'd you kiss me?"

"I didn't. The dog did," she said.

Thor licked Oliver's face.

"Oh, man," said Oliver, pulling his head out.

"You know what that boy needs?" said Robby. "A girlfriend."

Oliver was heading down the hallway at school, fixing lockers, when Miley came up to him. "Oliver, see that girl over there?" she said. "She thinks you're cute."

"Too bad I'm already cruisin' down the Hannah Highway," Oliver replied.

Oliver, you need a real girlfriend.

Maybe you two should go out sometime!

You mean, go out with HER?
You mean, go out with HIM?

Oh, Hannah, I love you. Even with gum on your face.

That's your "I've-got-a-sneaky-idea" look!

You'll always be "Smokin' Oken" to me.

Miley spotted Lilly and pulled her over. "Hey, what about Lilly?!" she asked Oliver. "You guys would be perfect together."

"Excuse me?" said Lilly.

Oliver went to his locker. Inside was a picture of Hannah.

"Soon, my love, we'll be together," Oliver said.

Chad smushed a wad of gum on the picture of Hannah, then walked away.

Oliver ripped off the ruined picture. Underneath was the exact same photo. "Hello, again," he said.

Lilly smiled slyly.

"I know that look," said Miley. "You have a great idea."

At the beach Lilly was hiding behind a large rock.

"I came as fast as I could!" said Oliver, breathless. "Is she still here?"

"Right down there," said Lilly, pointing.

"I can't believe you saw Hannah Montana break up with her boyfriend right here on our beach," said Oliver.

Look, I'm in love with you. Forever.

How could I think that guy was Hannah?

"Good luck, Oliver," said Lilly as she left. "If things don't work out, you're still Smokin' Oken."

Oliver approached a woman who was sitting with her back to him.

"Hi, it's me, Oliver," said Oliver. "I heard about your breakup and I'm here for you."

The woman turned around—and turned out to be a guy.

Oliver went over to another person sitting close by. "Hannah?" he said.

Miley, wearing her Hannah wig and sunglasses, turned around. She was chewing an enormous wad of bubble gum.

Hannah, is that really you?

"You're the kid from the moonroof," said Miley, drooling. "Look at you, all upside right. Want some gum?"

You look like you could use a chew, too.

OMG! Are you chewing gum?

Yep, GUM! I just LOVE GUM!

"I didn't know you liked gum," said Oliver.

"Oh, I'm a chewer all right," said Miley, chewing loudly in his face.

Soon her mouth started to turn black. "It's licorice," she explained. She blew a black bubble that got bigger and bigger. The bubble burst and Oliver's face was covered.

"How do you like me now?" Miley asked.

"I...I...still love you!" said Oliver.

"What more do I have to do?" Miley exploded. "You and Hannah Montana are never, ever gonna be together."

BLACK gum! It's the best! Just look at the bubble I can blow! Woo hoo!

Oliver, I've got something to tell you...

"Why not?' asked Oliver.

Miley took a deep breath. "Because..." she began. She took a quick look around the beach to make sure that they were alone. "I'm Hannah Montana. Me. Miley." Miley took off her disguise.

Oliver fainted.

"Okay, that went well," Miley said.

I'm...her. You know...Hannah. AND I'm Miley too.

After he recovered, Oliver asked, "How come you didn't tell me?"

"I'm sorry," said Miley. "Are we gonna be okay?"

"Yeah, we're okay," said Oliver.

They hugged and Miley said, "Let's go grab a hot dog."

I'm sorry. I didn't want to deceive you.

Ooo, ooo,
Itchy Woman

Indoor plumbing is a good thing.

"Okay, people, it's pop quiz time!" Mr. Picker called out.

The class moaned.

"First question," said Mr. Picker. "Who can tell me why this is the worst day of my life?" he asked. "I'm the chaperone of this year's class camping trip. Twenty-four glorious hours without indoor plumbing."

"Ewwww!" Amber and Ashley said together.

"Come on, guys, think about it," said Miley. "Sittin' under the stars, breathing all that fresh mountain air, surrounded by the sounds of nature."

Gee, Mr. Picker, camping's not so bad.

There's the stars, 'n fresh air, 'n...did I mention the stars yet?

Losers!

Ooooeooh!

Amber and Ashley turned to Miley and Lilly. "Losers. Oooh." Then they touched fingers and made the sizzle sound.

"Did I mention the four of you will be sharing the same tent?" said Mr. Picker.

"What?" the four girls cried.

We're sharing WHAT with WHO??!

The next day Miley came down the stairs in her pajamas. She used a red marker to dot her face and arms, then coughed loudly to get her father's attention.

"Honey, you really look terrible," said Robby.

"Couldn't sleep," Miley rasped. "Feel sick."

Robby put his hand up to her forehead. "I'll just have to cancel that interview I set up for Hannah Montana and Taylor Kingsford."

He reached for the phone, and Miley jumped up to stop him.

"Taylor Kingsford?!" she cried. "He's the coolest VJ on TV!"

Caught, Miley coughed again.

Are you sure you're sick, Miley? Looks like no interview on the Kingsford show today.

THIS is the BATHROOM???

Watch out for the Miley-cat. Vicious!

Robby gave her a look. "Miley, I know you don't want to share a tent with Amber and Ashley on the camping trip, but I want you to promise me you'll be the better person," he said.

"Okay, fine," Miley said.

"That's my girl," said Robby.

At the campsite Oliver pointed a video camera toward himself. "It was the sixth day without food," he said in an Australian accent.

"That is so not funny anymore," said Miley as he turned the camera toward her.

Oliver jiggled the camera and cried, "It's the Malibu Miley Cat! Very rare, very vicious!"

"Okay, people, set up your tents," called out Mr. Picker.

Miley went over to Amber and Ashley.

"Okay, I know we've had our problems," Miley said. "But whaddya say we put up this tent, make a fire, and cook us up a big pot of friendship?" asked Miley.

Gee, we'd like to chat, but we gotta go wash our clothes down at the crick.

HOW does this go together?

Cookin' up a big pot of friendship!

"Well, we'd like to, but we don't speak Hillbilly," said Ashley.

"You know what I'm thinking, Ash?" said Amber.

"Half-caff—" said Ashley.

"Non-fat latte," said Amber.

Lilly, don't!

As Amber and Ashley left, Lilly pulled out a slingshot and aimed it at them. Miley swung her off aim. The sling shot released—and Mr. Picker grabbed his rear end.

"Ta-daa!" said Miley, 30 minutes later.

Lilly stared at the fully assembled tent. "How did you do that?" she asked.

At that moment Amber and Ashley returned.

Uh-oh, sorry Mr. Picker!

"And we're supposed to sleep in this?" said Amber, touching the tent material. "It's synthetic!"

"Ewwww!" said Amber and Ashley.

Mr. Picker approached and Amber said, "Yoo-hoo, Mr. Picker?"

"Did we build ours the right way?" asked Ashley.

Ta-daaaaah! I put up this tent all by myself.

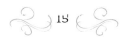

Look, Mr. Picker, we put up this tent all by ourselves.

Oh, no, you didn't.

Mr. Picker, they're taking credit for our work! Make them stop!

"Wow, I'm impressed," said Mr. Picker.

"But Miley put up that tent!" said Lilly. "They just went for lattes!"

"Lattes?" asked Amber.

"In the forest?" added Ashley.

"Why don't you just apologize to each other?" said Mr. Picker.

"We're sorry...that you are two lying evil nasties!" said Lilly.

Mr. Picker ordered Miley and Lilly to do the dishes. As Ashley put her plate into the tub, she deliberately knocked over the stack of clean plates. "Oops, sorry," she said. "See? I can apologize."

Awww! Too bad you've got SO many dishes to wash!

Last straw time! Let's get 'em.

Why does beauty sleep look so scary?

What was that sound? Sure was loud.

Later that night Miley, Lilly, Amber and Ashley were snuggled in their sleeping bags when they heard a rustling sound outside the tent.

"What was that?" Amber whispered. "Ashley...Ashley!"

They heard a low growl. Something shook the tent.

"It could be a bear," said Miley. "Or a mountain lion."

"Whatever it is, it sounds hungry," said Lilly.

There came more growls, and something punched the tent.

Miley got out of her sleeping bag. "Wish me luck," she

You go first. I'm prettier.

Could be lions. Or tigers...

...or bears. Oh gee!

Thanks, Oliver! We scared 'em good!

Look at them go! Yee-ha!

whispered. "Our only hope is if I can get to the ranger station alive."

Outside the tent, Miley joined Oliver, who was holding a big stick.

"Thanks," Miley whispered.

They started to grunt and moan, pretending to struggle.

Miley's head appeared through a slit in the tent.

"Lilly, he's got me!" said Miley.

"Oh no, he doesn't!" Lilly said, grabbing Miley. But the two of them were pulled out of the tent.

Outside, Miley, Lilly and Oliver pounded on the tent. Amber and Ashley came flying out of the front, screaming. They raced straight into the port-a-potty. It rocked back and forth and fell over.

Timmmberrrrr!

Photo op!

See another side of me!

Hey, everybody, let's hear it for Hannah!

"Ewwww!" Amber and Ashley cried from inside.

Miley, Lilly and Oliver celebrated with high-fives as they crawled out of the bushes. Lilly pulled out her camera phone and took Miley's picture in front of the port-a-potty.

The next day Hannah Montana was taping a show with Taylor Kingsford when her cell phone rang. "Hey, Oliver? I'm kinda busy," she said, scratching her arm absentmindedly.

"Remember that bush we were hiding in?" Oliver asked. He was covered in calamine lotion. "It was poison oak!"

Poison oak? Uh-oh...

What's...with...this...itching?

I've got a new dance!

Here's my itchy-scratchy partner, Lola!

During the interview Miley tried not to scratch, but the itching was getting worse.

Miley grabbed Lilly-disguised-as-Lola from offstage and pulled her on camera.

"I call it the 'scratch dance!'" said Miley. "Contagious, isn't it?"

"'Scratch dancin'!" Miley and Lilly sang together.

Later at home, Miley sat with Robby and Jackson watching the broadcast.

"I can't watch this," said Miley, covering her eyes with her hand mitts.

"You don't have to," said Robby. "I'm recordin' it!"

Folks, you never know what Hannah is up to!

I can't look. I can't LOOK!

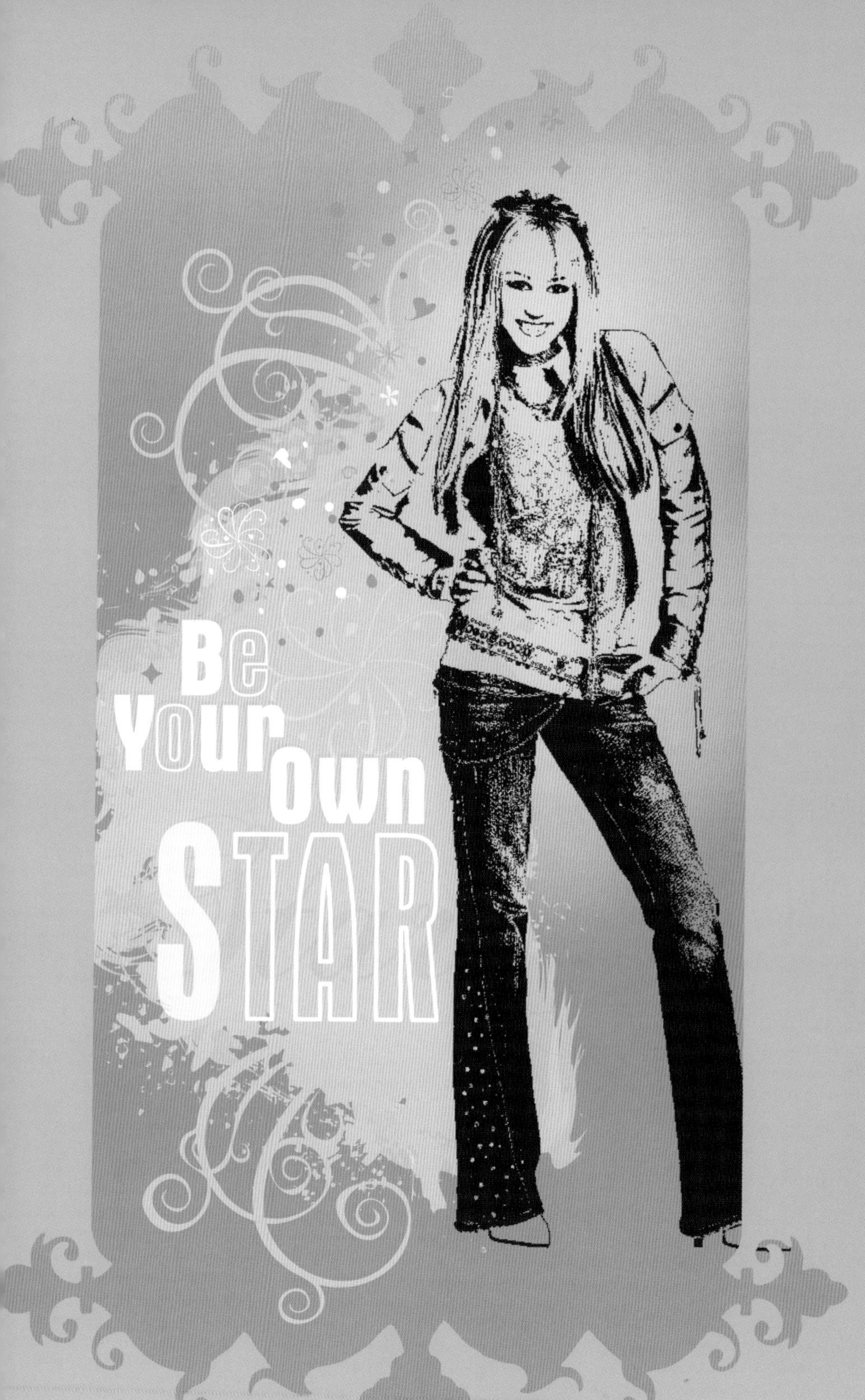
Be
Your own
STAR

Just Like You

So what you see
is only half the story.
There's another side of me
I'm the girl you know
but I'm someone else too.
If you only knew.

It's a crazy life
but I'm alright.

(chorus)
I got everything I've always wanted.
Living the dream.
So yeah, everything I've always wanted
isn't always what it seems.
I'm a lucky girl
whose dreams came true.
But underneath it all
I'm just like you

Don't wanna be treated differently
I wanna keep it all inside.
Half the time I've got my name in lights
The other half I'm by your side.

It's a crazy life
but I'm just fine.

(chorus)
Can't you see
I'm just an ordinary girl?
Living in an extra-ordinary world.
Trying to live
trying to learn
trying to just be who I am
who I am.

(chorus x 2)
But underneath it all
I'm just like you